The text of this book is set in Vollkorn point 14

Book design by M.E.R

Cover design and illustrations by Amanda Coakley

Dedicated to

Lucy,
for always helping me find the next great adventure

The Buttercup Series began as a bedtime story. This project would not have been possible without you. You inspired me to stretch my imagination to marvelous heights; I will forever be grateful.

The Buttercup Adventures
Volume One:
The Glass Frog

by M.E.R

A Fortune for a Penny

The city of Amalease is the safest place on earth. It is surrounded by large green trees that keep the busy city within and the endless dry desert outside. At its center is a giant castle where the King and Queen live. They create fair laws that make sure cruel people are exiled from the city.

Ten years ago the King and Queen had a daughter. The Queen, because of her love of butter, named her Buttercup, and what could be better than naming your child after your favorite food? Ironically, Princess Buttercup was born with yellow hair. It's almost as yellow as butter!

Most people want to remain safe within the city, protected from beasts and rude people, but Buttercup wants to go on adventures. She wants to leave and travel great distances to see wondrous new people and places. At the moment, the only adventures Buttercup can go on are those within the castle or city. She and her friend Hector race through the castle's many long hallways and up the tallest towers in search of adventures. Playing with Hector and deciding to grow her blond hair as long as possible are the only two things she likes about being a princess. Her mom, the Queen, makes her wear dresses and go to parties where she has to listen to older people talk about boring politics. She tells her she must listen nicely to others, even if she is not interested, and sit prettily with her hands folded in her lap. Buttercup would rather slouch in her seat, sigh nosily, and wear pants and a shirt, than learn how to be a proper princess.

Today, Buttercup is daydreaming of running through the castle with her friend Hector. She's not listening to her tutor, who is rambling on about the geography of the city. Since she is royal, she goes to school in the castle. Her tutor, Mr. Creaky, talks a lot and makes her read and write. He says big words she rarely understands, and his mustache is so large that it looks like some animal is hibernating under his nose for the winter.

"Buttercup?" Mr. Creaky grunts. His voice is deep and his accent makes it sound like he is saying Bu*dd*ercup instead of Bu*tt*ercup.

"Mmm?" she asks, afraid that he asked her an

important question.

"Lessons are done today," he says.

Her heart thuds with joy. School is over!

She jumps from her seat and runs from the room. The papers in her hands catch the wind and flutter behind her. Buttercup does not pick up her schoolwork, instead she scoops up a shiny penny that winks in the candle light. She slips the penny in her dress pocket and continues skipping down the hallway. She has already forgotten what Mr. Creaky tried to teach her about geography.

Buttercup tiptoes through the castle, as silent as the mice that scurry behind the walls. She goes down the creakiest stairs and doesn't make a sound.

She peeks around the corner. The kitchens are busy with workers as they prepare lunch. The chef's cat sleeps in the corner with one eye open. Chester is always looking for mice, but Buttercup doesn't think he needs to eat any more. He is already the fattest cat in all of Amalease.

Buttercup dashes into the room and grabs a fresh baked roll off a baking sheet. She stuffs it in her mouth, slips through a door and out into the sunshine.

She sees Hector. He's the stable boy and her

best friend. They grew up playing games together on the castle grounds. In the spring, they'd slide through mud puddles and throw mud balls. Buttercup's mother put a stop to those games years ago, so now Buttercup and Hector enjoy exploring the castle and town.

Hector is a little taller than her, with short black hair and a large nose. Buttercup jokes that he can smell everything. Hector jokes that Buttercup is going to trip on her hair if it grows any longer.

Buttercup, still on her tip toes, stops behind him and says, "Hello."

"AH!" Hector jumps.

Buttercup giggles. He's jumpy when it comes to surprises, yet when he sees something scary, such as when Chester is eating a dead mouse, he simply backs away slowly.

"What are you up to?" she asks him.

"I'm just brushing the horses. After I'm done, I'm going to the fair, want to come?"

Buttercup has never been to the fair before. It comes every year to the city square, but her parents are always too busy to take her. Her tutor, Mr. Creaky, says that most people go to see the sport competitions. She puts her hand in her dress pocket and grips the shiny penny. Buttercup wonders what she could buy with it.

"Okay!" she agrees. "It sounds like a wonderful adventure!"

When Hector is done with his chores he saddles two horses, and they gallop to the town square.

Buttercup falls in love with the fair. The city square and all the other sidewalks are decorated with colorful chalk drawings. Children race this way and that picking up chalk and adding more bright images to the dull brown walkways. There are red and orange streamers crisscrossing above the tents. People yell from one side of the square to the other, calling out names, goods, and prices. A few jugglers on stilts walk by. One juggles flowers. He reaches down and slides a white daisy through her blond braid.

"Thank you." Buttercup smiles.

They keep walking. Hector watches an archery contest where men with strong muscular arms pull on bowstrings and shoot arrows at a target. They pass a large open field where men challenge each other to a duel. At first Buttercup is afraid someone might get hurt, but Hector explains that they fight for fun. He points to their swords and shows her they're made of wood. The men even wear padding to protect themselves. After watching a few duels they leave in search of something else. Hector finds a group of children playing marbles. He joins them and wins a few games before losing against a boy who is younger, yet twice Hector's size. He shakes the boys hand and then leaves with Buttercup. He grumbles as they weave through the crowds. Buttercup ignores him. He can sometimes be a sore loser.

They walk through the market, where tents of all different colors sell various foods. Hector stops at a lavender colored tent.

"Look." He points to the tent's sign, which is a painting of an old lady. "She's a fortune teller."

Buttercup reads the words under the picture, "A penny for a fortune." She smiles at Hector and pulls out the penny from her pocket. "I'm going to get my fortune told."

Hector follows her inside. An old lady sits in a squeaky rocking chair with a shawl over her shoulders. Her light blue eyes are on Buttercup. "Are you the one looking for a fortune?"

"Oh, yes!" Buttercup sits down and the old lady closes her eyes and rocks in her chair.

"Ah, I see you love adventures." The old lady stops rocking. The smile leaves her face. "Tomorrow you will find something important. It will bring you closer to your destiny. Be careful on your journey, you will face those who wish to stop you." She opens her eyes and takes hold of Buttercup's hand. "Be careful my dear."

As they leave the tent Buttercup's heart skips with joy.

"What was she talking about?" Hector asks once they are back in the city square.

Buttercup shrugs and smiles. "I'm not sure, but she said I would be going on an adventure!" Her dream is going to come true. Her excitement makes it easy to ignore the old lady's warning of danger.

Together they watch more sport competitions. One woman is so strong she holds three people in the air while balancing on a ball. They stay to watch falcon races and many other performances. They are having so much fun, they lose track of time and soon realize the sun is going down. However, before they leave, they buy a loaf of fresh baked bread and then jump on their horses.

They race each other back to the castle, laughing. Hector's horse is faster, and he beats her to the castle gates.

"Mom! Dad!" Buttercup smiles and dismounts from her horse. "Hector took me to the fair!"

They don't seem happy, though.

The Queen wears a red cloak over her gown, and her golden crown sparkles in the fading sunlight. She waves a finger at Buttercup. "You should have told us where you had gone," she says sternly.

"Sorry, Mom," Buttercup says, and then she smiles. "You have to try this bread!"

Before her mom can say anything, Buttercup puts a huge piece of bread in her mouth.

The Queen's eyes grow wide as she chews the enormous clump. She nods and says, "Mmmaugrg."

Buttercup covers her mouth with her hand, but she cannot hold in her laughter. It escapes through her fingers. Soon her dad and Hector join in and all of them laugh enthusiastically.

The Hidden Trunk

In the morning Buttercup braids her hair. It's Saturday, which means no school and no dresses! She is only allowed to wear pants on the weekends; every other day she has to wear annoying, itchy dresses! She excitedly changes out of her nightgown and puts on her exploring clothes: pants and a shirt.

Buttercup opens her bedroom door and goes down to the kitchen. After sneaking away with breakfast, she tiptoes through hallways. She climbs down spiral staircases and up spiral staircases. She opens doors and then forgets to close them.

She comes to an old wooden door marked 355.

She frowns. She has never seen a door in the castle with a number on it.

Her heart pounds with excitement and fear as her fingers grip the door knob and twist. It opens, and behind is a set of stairs that travel down into a pitch black room.

Buttercup smiles a secret smile. She has found something special, she is sure of it! The best part it is that no one helped her. She found it all by herself.

She holds the handrail and slowly climbs down the dark stairs. On the last step, she feels something against her toe. Reaching down, she finds matches and a candle. After lighting it, Buttercup can see the room.

She is in a cellar. She did not know the castle had a cellar!

There are shelves lined with old jars, old china, and moth-eaten linens. Cobwebs hang from the ceiling, and she brushes them away as she walks in.

There is only one thing in the center of the room on the floor. It's as if someone wanted it to be found. It's an old chest.

Buttercup kneels down. It's made of wood and framed with thick metal. There are no locks. She finds the lid and tries to open it. She grunts and pulls, but it's no use. It's rusted shut.

She races back up the stairs and through the hallways. The wind blows the candle out.

"Hector!" Buttercup calls as she runs into the stables.

A head pops up from behind one of the horse stalls.

"Why are you holding a candle?" he asks, frowning.

She ignores his question and asks excitedly, "Do you have a tool that could open something?"

"Yeah," Hector reaches down and then holds something up. "Would nippers, do?"

"What?"

He comes closer and shows her. Buttercup thinks they look like giant plyers someone might use to pull a tooth out. She shivers just thinking about it.

Hector says, "I use them to trim horse hooves. They could open something, I think."

"How about something that's rusted shut?" Buttercup asks.

Hector shrugs. "Let's find out."

Buttercup leads the way, and Hector follows. After getting lost and retracing her steps, she eventually finds the door numbered 355.

They climb down the stairs, and Buttercup lights the candle.

"Over there." She points to the metal chest.

Hector fits the flat ends of the nippers under the lip of the chest. He grunts, pulling with all his weight. There's a loud *CRACK*, and the chest pops open.

"Oh!" Buttercup exclaims. She kneels next to Hector and reaches inside. She pulls out a...frog?

Hector shrieks and jumps back, "A frog!"

Buttercup laughs. "It's not real! It's made of glass."

"Oh, yeah," Hector chuckles nervously and waves a hand. "I wasn't scared."

"ROAR!" Buttercup shoves the glass frog in Hector's face. He jumps again, stumbles backward, and lands in the chest. The lid swings shut.

The chest ate him!

Buttercup quickly lifts the lid and is relieved to see Hector sitting inside. He's holding a large old book.

Her heartbeat slows. He's safe. Buttercup puts her hands on her hips. "I thought the chest ate you!"

Hector laughs. "Nope, but I found a book!" he says with a smile.

Buttercup helps him out and then starts climbing the stairs.

"Where are you going?"

"I want to show my Dad!" she says lifting the glass frog.

"But –"

Buttercup doesn't listen to what he has to say. She can only think of the glass frog and what it means. She wants to know, she needs to know. It must be important, it just must!

Hector is running after her, but she's faster.

She reaches the throne room where she finds her parents sitting on their thrones. Her dad wears his colossal red robe and spiky golden crown.

They are listening to the needs of the people from the city, who come up to the throne, one at a time, to ask for something and present gifts.

Finally the King calls for a break. Buttercup sprints up the stairs and sticks the glass frog under his nose.

"What's this?" she asks.

He laughs.

She does not understand why he is laughing. She frowns. "What is it?"

The King smiles. "That, my dear, has a story. I believe you are old enough now to hear it. So I shall tell it to you. Tonight, when you are all tucked in bed I will tell you the history of our family."

Magical Powers

Buttercup can barely contain her excitement. Her heart beats fast in her chest. She rubs her fingers together and then bites her fingernails.

"Please stop," Hector says, "You are making me nervous!"

Buttercup huffs.

"What are you nervous about, anyway?" Hector asks, raising his eyebrows.

She looks at him with wide eyes. "I'm excited *and* nervous! What do you think dad is going to tell me?"

"I don't know." Hector widens his eyes, too.

Buttercup raises her eyebrows higher. She leans towards him but it doesn't cause him to blink.

He narrows his eyes.

She narrows her eyes, too.

They stare at each other for many minutes.

Finally, Hector begins to smile and then he blinks.

"I win!" Buttercup throws her hands up and laughs.

He rolls his eyes.

There's a knock on the door.

Buttercup's stomach does a flip. She grips the glass frog tightly in her hands. Her dad is going to tell them what it all means. They're going to solve a real mystery!

"Come in," Buttercup says.

The King opens the door and steps inside.

"Buttercup and Hector," he says with a smile. "How are you?"

"Good." Buttercup bounces on the bed. "Dad, it's story time!"

Her father smiles. "Yes, that's right." He sits next to her and starts the story.

"You've found the key to your powers." He taps the glass frog that is in her lap. "This frog holds the key. That book," he points to the one Hector holds, "has all your answers."

Buttercup frowns and puts her hands on her hips. "Dad, that wasn't even a story. It doesn't make any sense. Are you talking a different language?"

He laughs a booming laugh and tips his head back.

She doesn't like that he's laughing at her, so she doesn't laugh with him. She is silent, and finally he answers her question.

"Well, Buttercup, let me start from the beginning. You are only the seventh royal in the family to be a girl. All the other children have been boys."

She interrupts him, "But what about Mommy?"

"She married into the family. That is different."

Buttercup wonders how that works, but before she can ask he continues.

"In the history books it is written that every royal girl from our family is born with magical powers. You're the first girl to be born in the royal family for many years. You, Buttercup, have magical powers."

Buttercup's eyes grow wide. She has magical powers?

Hector jumps off the bed. His brown eyes are

wide with fear.

"She has magical powers?" he asks fearfully, pointing to Buttercup. "AH! DON'T HURT ME! DON'T HURT ME!" Hector runs out of the room and into the hall waving his hands above his head. "DON'T HURT ME! DON'T HURT ME!"

Buttercup giggles. "Don't mind him," she tells her dad. "He can be strange sometimes, but he's my best friend."

Her dad smiles and then pats her head. "Buttercup, I know nothing about your powers. I can't help with this. You must go on the adventure by yourself, or," he pauses and holds her hand, "with Hector. He could help and give you some company. I'll tell Hector's boss that he'll be leaving for a little while. I'll get the castle another stable hand while he is away." He reaches out and gives her a hug only a dad can give. His long arms easily wrap around her, but her short arms barely hug his stomach. "Find your friend and explain that you don't have your powers yet. That might make him feel less scared about this whole situation. Afterward you can leave with Hector to go find your powers."

M.E.R

X Marks the Spot

Buttercup runs down hallways, crashes through doors, and climbs down stairwells. She grips the glass frog with both hands, careful not to drop it. Finally, she comes to the stables. Hector is running around, grabbing things and packing them into a saddle bag.

"Hector, what are you doing?" Buttercup asks.

"AH!" He drops what he is holding, and it lands on his foot. He hops up and down. "OW!"

Buttercup rushes to help him, but he pushes her away.

"Hector, I'm trying to help you!"

"No," he says, taking a step back. "Go away! Don't hurt me with your magic stuff!"

"But I don't have magic! Not now, anyway."

He stops packing his bag and looks at her with his big brown eyes, "You don't?"

"No." Buttercup reaches down and picks up the hammer he dropped. "A hammer?" she laughs.

"What were you going to do with a hammer?"

He doesn't answer her question, but says, "So, you're not going to hurt me with your magic?"

Buttercup shakes her head. "Of course not. And even if I did have magical powers, I wouldn't hurt you. You're my best friend."

"Really?"

She nods. "Of course."

Hector reaches out and gives her a hug. He squeezes so hard that all the air leaves her lungs.

"Uh...Hec...tor...can't...breathe..."

"What?" He pulls away. "I can breathe, what are you talking about?"

Buttercup gulps in air. "Not you, me! You almost squeezed all the air out of me."

"Oh! Sorry."

Once Buttercup has enough air in her lungs she asks, "Would you like to come with me and help me figure out my power?"

Hector jumps up. "Yes! Yes I would!" He turns and begins leaving the stables.

"Where are you going?"

He turns back around. "To tell my boss. I can't just leave the castle."

"My dad said he would tell your boss and find another stable hand."

"Oh!" He smiles and makes his way back to Buttercup. He digs into his saddle bag and pulls out the old book he found in the chest. "Well, I guess we should start planning. I bet there's something that could help us in here."

They sit in the hay and flip through the pages.

"Buttercup, look!" Hector points to a page.

It is a beautiful old map with a small black X on one side. There are drawings of trees, mountains, lakes, oceans, and castles. A giant green sea serpent is in one of the oceans, and the compass at the top is drawn as a bowl with a fish in it.

"Whoa!" Buttercup sees a castle in the map that looks familiar. She points, "That's Amalease, where we live."

Hector looks at the map for a long time before saying, "I think we need to somehow get to the X."

Buttercup nods. "My dad said he couldn't help us. He doesn't know anything about how to get my powers. He said I would have to travel to find them. Do you think if we go to that X I'll get my magic?" Buttercup hugs the glass frog to her chest.

Hector shrugs. "It's our best option. We should go there and find out."

The glass frog suddenly starts to glow. Hector jumps away, sending the book flying into a pile of hay. Buttercup gasps and almost falls backwards as she leans away from the glowing frog.

Buttercup stutters, "I - I didn't do anything. It started glowing all by itself." As she looks at the bright white light she wonders out loud, "Do you think it does that when we make a good decision?"

"Mmm," Hector thinks. "Maybe it glows when we are getting closer to the X."

"Maybe," Buttercup says. "Then we should leave soon and get to the X."

This is it! An adventure to discover her hidden powers! She never thought she would ever go on a real adventure! Now she is. She and Hector are going on a journey all by themselves!

Smiling, Buttercup stands. "I'm going to get food and water. Can you pack everything and get the horses ready?"

"Sure thing, Buttercup." Hector stands and rushes about the stables, collecting items and saddling two horses.

Buttercup sprints through the castle, gathering food, clothes, and water. After getting everything they will need she meets Hector back in the stables.

The horses are ready.

Buttercup mounts one horse and holds the reigns. Her horse looks like a cow. It is white with black splotches. Each spot is shaped differently; one looks a little like a duck. Its mane is completely black, but its tail has some white hair mixed in. Hector's horse is grey, even its mane and tail, and there are a few darker spots on its neck.

As she sits on her horse, Buttercup suddenly feels sad and anxious. Her stomach is filled with butterflies. She's leaving home. She's leaving everything she knows.

Hector can see Buttercup is afraid. He tries to reassure her. "Buttercup, we'll be back."

She turns to her friend and smiles a sad smile. "You promise?"

"Of course." He crosses his heart with a finger. "Now, what are you going to name your horse?"

Buttercup raises her eyebrows. "It doesn't have a name?"

"Well, you can give it a different one."

"Oh." She thinks for a moment. "Her name is Forget-Me-Not. I'm naming her after the flower."

Hector laughs. "That's a strange name, but I like it." He spurs his horse forward. A moment later he turns around and starts to say, "Why would you – "

SMACK!

Hector hits his head on the stable roof and falls from his horse.

"Hector!" Buttercup jumps off Forget-Me-Not and kneels next to him. "Are you hurt?"

"Ow...my head..." He rubs his forehead.

"Why didn't you duck under the roof?" Buttercup asks.

"I was confused at the name you gave your horse. It's so long! You can't even shorten it, otherwise her name would be 'Forget Me' or 'Forget' or 'Me' or 'Not', and all of those words don't make for a good name..."

Buttercup laughs. "Well, I like the name."

"Okay, okay. Fine. Forget-Me-Not it is," Hector agrees.

"What's the name of your horse?" Buttercup asks.

"Windthrup." He smiles. "Because he flies like the wind."

Buttercup laughs and helps Hector to his feet.

After they get back on their horses, they duck their heads under the stable roof. They travel through the city square, where just the other day they played with children and watched all the festivities. No one is playing in the square today. Instead, it is filled with people buying food for the day.

Hector and Buttercup gallop along the road until they come to the gate of the city. Beyond the gate is the desert with its endless miles of sand. As they travel through it at a slow pace, Buttercup turns one last time and watches the castle disappear behind them. She is afraid of leaving home and doesn't know when she will be back. She is glad to have her friend with her, but Buttercup already misses her parents and the castle.

She gathers her strength and turns her back on the city of Amalease. She squints against the sun as they travel deeper into the desert.

She is sad, but also excited. They are going on an adventure without adults! She and Hector are taking on the world.

The Oasis

Buttercup and Hector have been riding through the desert for what feels like weeks, but Hector says it has only been four days. The desert feels endless. If the wind picks up just a little sand gets in her eyes. When that happens she burrows her face into Forget-Me-Not's mane of black hair. Buttercup is pretty sure they are the only living things out here. She hasn't seen any insects or small critters or even another person.

On the first night Buttercup cried before falling asleep. She missed home so much that she cried on the second night too, but after that she had no more tears. Hector keeps telling her that they'll return to the city. She knows they will, but this is the first time she has ever left home. Everything around her looks and feels so different. She has gone on short trips before, but she was always with her parents and they never let her out of their sight. This time it is just herself and Hector. She misses her parents more than anything. It's a deep ache in her chest. No matter what she does, the ache does not go away.

A few nights ago, while lying on her blanket, she wondered if she still liked adventures. So far she had gotten sand in her face and missed home so much her chest hurt. Before she closed her eyes Buttercup wondered if her dreams of adventure were simply just dreams that could never come true.

"Buttercup," Hector turns in his saddle. "Can I have a loaf of bread?"

She nods and opens the saddle bag. She searches inside, but her hands only find air.

She can't believe it. The bag is empty! They ate all their food!

"Hector, this is bad!" she calls out.

He stops. Windthrup nods his head and swishes his tale from side to side. Forget-Me-Not pauses next to Windthrup.

She keeps searching the bag, but there is no food. She starts to panic.

"There's no food! Hector, we're DOOMED! We're going to STARVE!"

Hector is not despaired by this news. He is smiling and pointing straight ahead.

In the distance, there is a patch of green and a shimmer of blue, with palm trees rising out behind sand dunes. The blue belongs to a small lake of fresh water.

Buttercup squeals, "We're saved!" She spurs Forget-Me-Not forward. They race down and up sand dunes and reach the trees as the sun lowers in the sky.

"An oasis," Hector says smiling.

"A what?" Buttercup asks.

"Oasis," he repeats. "A place that has water and plants in the middle of a desert."

Buttercup slides down from Forget-Me-Not. She gathers the rope and leads her horse to the water. Forget-Me-Not drinks while Buttercup kneels and scoops the crystal clear water into her hands. She drinks so much that she feels it sloshing around in her stomach.

Hector and Windthrup have a drink, too.

When they're finished, Buttercup and Hector sprint through the sand and into the cluster of palm trees. Even though they are exhausted from their long days of travel, they have a little energy left. They use it all up running through the palm trees and playing hide and go seek.

After Hector wins, Buttercup lies down under all the different types of trees. Hector does the same.

They gaze up at the light blue sky and watch as the stars start to shine. It's dusk, Buttercup's favorite time of day. It's when all the heat is replaced by cool breezes, twinkling stars, and a bright moon.

"Look!" Hector points straight up.

He is pointing to something that hangs from one of the tress. It's round.

He stands, reaches up, and picks it.

"Fruit!" Hector exclaims.

Buttercup's stomach growls. They found food!

Together, they go from tree to tree collecting fruit and munching on it. There are peaches, plums, apricots, cherries, and even almonds. They fill their bags with the food and then roll out their bed mats.

"I think it's strange," Hector says before they fall asleep.

"What?" Buttercup asks.

"This oasis. I didn't know these types of fruits grew in the desert. What if this place is bad? What if we just ate poisonous fruit?"

Buttercup frowns. "I hope not. I guess we'll

find out in the morning."

"AH!" Hector scrunches up his face in fear. "I don't like that idea…"

Buttercup tries to reassure him. "Nothing tasted horrible. I think we're safe."

Soon, loud snoring fills the air. Buttercup turns and finds Hector asleep. She rolls her eyes. Wasn't he just scared about poisonous fruit? How could he then fall asleep so quickly? Buttercup sighs from confusion and exhaustion. Soon she is asleep too.

The City Of Ginglebop

The sunshine wakes them up the next morning. They pack quickly and fill their waterskins. At the castle, her parents only let her use waterskins when they went on trips. Now, she gets to use these skinny leather water pouches every day. Buttercup takes one last drink before they set off across the dry desert.

They travel all day in the hot sun and never rest. Finally, when both Buttercup and Hector are so tired they're almost falling off their horses and the sun is setting behind a distant sand dune, they come to something huge. It is so massive that they stop and stare at it for many minutes.

It's a stone wall. It's taller than a giraffe and smooth, so they won't be able to climb it. Buttercup looks to the left and right only to find the wall continues in both directions for miles. They won't be able to walk around it.

"What do we do?" Buttercup asks.

Hector jumps down from his horse and opens

M.E.R

his saddle bag. He pulls out the book they found in the chest.

Buttercup jumps off Forget-Me-Not and pulls out the glass frog.

"The wall doesn't end," Hector says, looking at the map.

"Mmm." Buttercup taps the glass frog. "We can't go around it, and we can't go over it. We definitely can't go through it."

"Why not?" Hector asks. He puts the book in his bag, and marches to the wall.

"What are you doing?" Buttercup calls, but he doesn't hear her. He just keeps walking. He walks right into the wall.

SMACK!

Buttercup runs to him. "What did you do that for? You know you can't walk through walls!"

Hector groans and rubs his head. "I thought it might not be there and that we were dreaming it."

Buttercup sighs. "Please don't do something like that again. You could hurt yourself!"

Hector nods. "Fine, but how are we going to get past this wall?"

"I need to think..." Buttercup holds the glass frog and thinks, thinks, thinks. What to do? What to do? And then she knows. "We have to go under it!"

"Under it?" Hector asks, his eyes wide. "That means we have to – "

"DIG!" Buttercup yells.

Suddenly there is a bright white light.

Buttercup gasps and almost drops the glass frog. Inside there is a swirling white mist that holds the light.

Hector gasps too. "I guess that's what we have to do! DIG!"

She sets the frog aside and starts digging. Hector helps. The horses copy Hector and Buttercup. They paw at the ground, digging too.

The sun has gone down completely. The light the frog emits radiates out so they can see. Soon the hole is big enough to crawl through.

"I feel something!" Buttercup calls out. Her fingers have found grass! She pushes the sand out of the way. "I think I can fit through!"

She crawls underneath and pulls herself through the gap, stands up and then sees – a knight in armor is pointing a sword at her chest.

"Who goes there?" the knight asks in a booming voice.

Buttercup takes a deep breath and says confidently, "I am Princess Buttercup from the city of Amalease."

"Oh!" the knight says. He puts his sword down. "I am sorry for pointing this at you, my Lady. You are most welcome to the city of Ginglebop. What may I do to help you?"

Buttercup wants to laugh. That name is so funny – Ginglebop – but she must be nice and hold back her laughter. She says, "Thank you."

There is a loud grunt and Buttercup and the knight turn to look behind them. Hair, arms, and fingers have appeared from underneath the wall. Hector! He crawls out and stands next to them.

He sighs, "Well, that was fun." Then he sees the knight and jumps back, "AH!"

"It's okay, he's a knight of Ginglebop and will help us," Buttercup tells him.

"A knight of who?"

"Ginglebop, it is the city you came to," the

knight says. "I'm not sure why you two came from *under* the wall." He points to part of the wall a few feet away. "That is the door."

Hector gawks at it, stunned. "Are you kidding me?" Hector says, "We just dug through a wall that had a door in it!"

Buttercup laughs.

Hector shakes out the sand from his hair and says in a tired voice, "I'll go get the horses...but this time I'm using the door."

The Glass Floor

Buttercup, the knight, and Hector stand in front of Ginglebop's Castle. It is gigantic with thousands of turrets and windows.

Buttercup says, "Wow, Mr. Knight! It's bigger than my castle in Amalease!"

The knight nods. "Thank you; however, please call me Knight Shire."

"Okay," Buttercup agrees.

Knight Shire opens the double-sided castle doors. Beyond is a huge empty entrance hall.

Buttercup steps inside, and her footsteps echo against the floor. She looks down and she almost loses her balance. She grabs hold of Hector, who stands behind her holding the horse's reins, and yells, "We're falling!"

Hector shakes his head. "No, we're not. The floor is made of glass."

Hector is right. They are not falling. The floor is solid, but they can see into the cellar. There are people below them. "Why are there people in the cellar of the castle?" Buttercup asks.

Knight Shire explains, "Well, our city market is below the castle. King Brandon built it so that thieves would be easier to catch."

Buttercup lets go of Hector. "Oh! That makes sense. It also looks beautiful."

They follow Knight Shire across the entrance hall. The horse's hooves make loud taps against the glass.

Knight Shire stops at a silver pedestal. Buttercup is just tall enough to see what sits on top of it. It's a small glass ball.

"What is that for?" Buttercup asks.

"Well, you see, that is our question too," Knight Shire says. "Our King has disappeared. On the night of his disappearance, this glass ball and pedestal appeared out of thin air. All the intelligent knights and all the intelligent ladies have come here to figure out what it means, but none of them can understand it."

Buttercup and Hector smile at each other. A mystery!

"The glass ball looks like your glass frog," Hector says, pulling out the frog from one of the saddle bags. He hands it to her.

Buttercup takes it. "You're right, it does!"

Suddenly there is a rumbling. It's so loud that Hector and Knight Shire cover their ears. Because Buttercup is holding the glass frog, she puts that against one of her ears and covers the other with her hand. The rumbling grows louder, and the glass floor begins to shake.

In the market square below, people are running. Some try to hide behind fruit stands, and others throw everything they are holding into the air and run.

"What is happening?" Buttercup yells over the noise. Her feet begin to wobble as the glass floor shakes. She fears it will break.

Knight Shire yells something, but she can't hear him. Suddenly he grabs both Hector and Buttercup's wrists and pulls them up a flight of stairs. Hector lets go of the horse's reins. They gallop around the entrance hall in fear, tossing their manes this way and that. Hector is so scared he begins yelling and throwing his arms everywhere, his eyes wide with terror. The rumbling has turned into a roar.

Knight Shire stops at the top of the stairs and looks out a giant window. He points to something, and Buttercup sees what is making all this commotion.

It's a dragon, but not a real one. It's made of random items. In the light of the moon, Buttercup can see its horns are bike handles. Its wings are connected coat hangers with cloth and a kite to make the skin. The spikes on its back are made from spoons, pencils, a brush, and a toothbrush. The scales on its chest are bright white dinner plates. Tied around the dragon's neck is a large apron decorated with the words, "Kiss the Cook." The front right knee cap is a giant turtle shell and one ankle is an old pocket watch. Its newspaper body is mostly white with a small chalkboard on the side of its belly. If that's not enough, one of its hips is made from a goldfish bowl that has a real live goldfish swimming inside! The dragon clenches its ice cream cone claws and opens its mouth wide. A jet of fire escapes. The three of them duck behind the wall.

"What type of dragon is that?" Buttercup yells, "What is going on?"

Knight Shire raises his voice above the noise. "The dragon appeared when our King left. It comes every night and tries to destroy the castle."

Hector's eyes are wide with fear, and he's shaking from head to toe.

That is when Buttercup gets an idea. The glass frog lights up. She wonders if this plan will work. It will put her in danger, but this might be the only way to save Ginglebop and themselves.

"That's it!" Buttercup yells.

She takes a deep breath and races down the stairs. She stops at the silver pedestal, reaches out and grabs the glass ball. Just like her frog, the glass ball lights up.

"Buttercup, what are you doing?" Hector yells, as he runs down the stairs.

"I think the king is the dragon! Or maybe the dragon ate the King!" Buttercup yells, "I don't know which, but I have to save him!"

"What?" Hector trips over his feet and falls to the glass floor. He scrambles up and calls after her,

"Are you crazy? It's going to eat you! NO! NO! NO! NO!"

Buttercup is not listening. She races across the glass floor, trying not to look down so as to keep her balance. She comes to the castle doors, throws them open, and runs outside.

The dragon is sitting on the front lawn of the castle. It roars loudly and fixes its button orange eyes on Buttercup.

The Dragon

Hector jumps onto his horse and races after Buttercup, but it's too late. The dragon has opened its mouth.

He can't believe what he is seeing. Buttercup walks right into the mouth of the dragon!

He yells and waves his arms. Maybe if he can get her attention, she'll run back out. However, Buttercup does not turn around – she simply walks deeper in until the darkness swallows her whole.

The dragon's tongue is squishy and wet. Buttercup lifts one of her shoes, and slime sticks to it.

"Ew!" she says.

All of a sudden the dragon closes its mouth. She's inside with no way to escape.

It's really dark and smells like rotten fish and moldy vegetables. Buttercup wants to plug her nose, but both her hands are full, one with the glass frog and the other with the glass ball.

The tongue flips upward, sending Buttercup

into the air. She screams! There is nothing to stop her from falling. She realizes too late that she's become dragon food!

SPLASH!

She lands in the dragon's stomach. It's like a giant swimming pool, but the liquid is green and sticky. The walls of the stomach glow a dark red. With that light she can just barely see.

"Where is the King?" Buttercup yells, and to her surprise someone answers.

"Here!"

She finds a man lying on a raft that floats on the green liquid.

"Are you the king?" Buttercup asks.

"No, I'm Mr. KingsFlesh. He's the king." He points to another man.

This other man is tied up with rope and sits on a raft as well, but he has a golden crown on his head.

"Then who are you?" Buttercup asks the man who is not tied up.

"I am the King's brother. This is my dragon. I made it out of paper and an assortment of other objects. I created it so that I could capture King

Brandon. I should have been king of Ginglebop, but my brother won the crown. Now I am destroying his city with this dragon and keeping him here so he cannot rule. I am the true King of Ginglebop!"

The dragon isn't real. Buttercup is relieved. She hadn't been eaten after all!

Two men say they are the King of Ginglebop, but only one can be. Which one is really the king? If she figures out who the king is then maybe the dragon will spit her out?

The glass frog lights up.

That's it! She has to determine who the true king is!

Mr. KingsFlesh watches as the glass frog begins to shine brighter and brighter. He points a shaking finger at her.

"You're a witch with great power!" he yells.

Buttercup decides to let him think that. She pretends she has magical powers and says, "That is right. These glass objects will light up when I say the true king's name. The one who is not the king of Ginglebop must leave the city and swear to never return or hurt the city ever again."

The two men nod in agreement because they are fearful of her powers.

Buttercup asks the glass ball and frog, "Is Mr. KingsFlesh the true king of Ginglebop?"

Nothing happens.

Mr. KingsFlesh begins to cry.

Then Buttercup asks, "Is –" She turns to the man who is tied up. "What is your name?"

"Brandon," he says.

"Is Brandon the true king of Ginglebop?"

The glass ball and frog light up.

Buttercup smiles. She found the true king!

Mr. KingsFlesh is still crying. His tears have collected on the floating raft and slowly they spill into the green liquid of the dragon's stomach.

Suddenly the liquid bursts into flames.

"Oh, no!" yells Buttercup. "We have to get out of here!"

"I can get us out! Help me!" King Brandon yells.

Buttercup swims over and hops onto the raft. She unties him.

He smiles at her and shakes out his hands and

legs. "It feels good to be free of that rope."

"That's great," Buttercup says quickly, "but we have something more important to think about." She points to the flames. "We're going to be burned!"

"Don't worry," says King Brandon, "The dragon will just throw us up."

"WHAT?" yells Buttercup, "Are you crazy? I don't want to be dragon puke!"

"Here we go!" King Brandon reaches over and presses a blue button on the side of the dragon's stomach that has EJECT written on it. Buttercup holds tightly to the raft. The stomach walls start closing in.

"AHA! We're going to be squished!" she yells.

But that doesn't happen. Instead, the green liquid sloshes around. The flames travel up the side of the stomach and now everything is on fire.

The dragon coughs, and the movement sends both rafts flying into the dragon's throat. It opens its mouth, and they travel out of the dragon and into the night.

Buttercup is screaming. They are hundreds of

feet above the ground! There is no way they are going to land without hurting themselves!

King Brandon presses a button on the raft, and it inflates into a giant sled. They hit the ground and slide to a stop.

They're safe! Buttercup stands on shaky legs. Her heart is beating fast against her chest.

POP!

They turn towards the sound.

The dragon has exploded. Buttercup ducks as a boomerang flies over her head, a beach ball bounces to the ground, plates crash around them, and a light bulb, hat, brush, pencil and bike handles sail overhead. The dragon has been destroyed.

Black Pirate Ice Cap

"Princess Buttercup!" Hector runs towards her. "What did you do? Why did you go into that dragon's mouth? How did that thing blow up? Who's this guy?" He points to Mr. KingsFlesh. "Who's that guy?" He points to King Brandon. "I don't know what is going on. This is so confusing!" Hector is so overwhelmed with everything that he faints.

Buttercup reaches out just in time and catches him. As she places him gently on the grass she sees his eyes are closed. It looks like he's sleeping.

"Mmm…" says Buttercup, "he should wake up soon."

Knight Shire asks, "What happened to the dragon?"

"Oh," Buttercup says, "It wasn't a real dragon. Mr. KingFlesh, the King's brother, created it to destroy Ginglebop because he wanted to be King. King Brandon was tied up in the dragon, and I saved him. Mr. KingsFlesh is now banished from Ginglebop."

"Wow!" says Knight Shire. "Thank you for your help. I'm glad you figured that out. It all sounds very confusing." Knight Shire walks to the stables while scratching his head in confusion. He saddles a castle horse and packs some food in a sack. After that is done he brings the horse over.

"Alright," says Mr. KingsFlesh as he mounts the horse. "I shall leave." He does not give his brother a hug nor does he wave goodbye. Buttercup knows he is still angry about not being the king of Ginglebop. She tries to not let that bother her. He was harming Ginglebop! He has to leave.

They watch as he turns and gallops into the sunset, never to return again.

The next morning Buttercup and Hector pack their belongings. They say goodbye to Knight Shire and King Brandon.

King Brandon gives Buttercup a hug and says, "As a token of our gratitude, please keep the glass ball."

"Really?" Buttercup smiles and gives him an

extra hug. "Thank you!" She places the glass ball in her saddle bag next to the food and water Knight Shire packed for them.

Together she and Hector thank them and then ride out of Ginglebop. As she turns to see the city one last time, she promises herself someday they will come back and visit.

It takes a whole day to ride across the dessert, but they do. Just before the sun sets, they come across something neither of them has ever seen.

"Wow!" says Buttercup. "It's huge!"

"Yeah," says Hector. "It's the largest swimming pool I've ever seen!"

Buttercup laughs. "No silly, it's an ocean! Mr. Creaky taught me about them in lessons, but I've never seen one!"

A long ship with three masts and six black sails is anchored near shore. Crew members of the ship walk the beach. They are packing wooden crates and tossing them onto the boat.

"Looks like they are about to leave," Hector says.

Buttercup pulls out the large book from one of

the saddle bags. She opens to the page with the map. The ocean is named Narwhal Ocean, and it looks so large and wide that in order to cross it they will need a boat!

She puts the book back, jumps off Forget-Me-Not, and marches towards the men.

"Excuse me," she says. "May I speak with your captain?"

One man raises an eyebrow, points and says gruffly, "Yes. He's right over there."

The captain is not pretty looking. He has an eye patch, one hook for a hand, two peg legs, and lots of scars on his face. Buttercup does not want to know how he got those scars, so she does not ask.

She takes a deep breath and looks the captain right in the eye. "My name is Buttercup, and I am the princess of the great city of Amalease. I ask for safe passage across these waters, please."

"Oh!" says the captain in a mocking tone. "Pleased to meet you; my name is Black Pirate Ice Cap. Welcome aboard our ship, The Ice Breaker."

Hands grab her around the waist. She's lifted off the ground and placed on the boat. More hands grab her, and then she finds herself tied to the center mast of the ship. She struggles, but there is no use.

She hears Hector yelling, and all at once he's tied up next to her.

Crew members are leading their horses onto the ship.

"AHHH!" Hector yells. "Pirates!"

She looks up and sees the flag waving in the wind at the top of the mast. It's black with a skull and cross bones. Buttercup realizes her mistake. She can't believe she didn't understand this was a pirate ship! They've been captured!

The boat hasn't moved yet. Maybe she can untie them and jump to shore.

Black Pirate Ice Cap yells, "Set sail!"

Oh no!

The crew members lift the anchor, and suddenly the shore is far away. They're out in the middle of the ocean!

Hector is still yelling like a maniac, "Pirates! PIRATES!" He is so terrified that he can't think of anything else to scream, but he keeps hollering in the hope that someone might find them. Soon

Hector is howling, "Blah! Blah! BLAH!!!!" because he can't think of anything else to yell.

Buttercup frowns. "Why are you bleating like a sheep?"

He doesn't hear her, but continues. "BLAH! BLAH! BLAH! BLAH!"

She sighs and rolls her eyes. What are they going to do now?

WAIT! Maybe there is an escape! The glass ball from Ginglebop is in her saddle bag, but she is still holding the glass frog. The pirates made a mistake by not taking it from her. She tightens her grip around it and makes sure no one is watching.

She needs something to cut through these ropes! She imagines a sharp object. The glass frog glows bright, and then a small piece of glass appears in her other hand.

She can't believe it worked. She knew the glass frog would light up when she made correct decisions, but she didn't know it could make things appear that she wished for! She saws at the rope with the sharp side of the glass.

"What are you doing?" Hector whispers. Then he sees the knife and yells, "Where did you get that?

Please cut FASTER; we need to escape!"

"Oh, no…" Buttercup mutters. All the pirates have heard Hector yelling. They turn and look at the two of them.

She works faster, and then the rope falls off. They are untied, but it's too late. The pirates are standing in front of them with swords pointed at their chests.

Frozen in place, they are petrified to move. It is then that Windtrup notices the swords. Hector's horse, out of fear, whinnies loudly and rears back on his hind legs. He kicks the air with his hoofs, and the pirates scatter back, afraid. Forget-Me-Not rears up too, and kicks at the pirates, who stumble and fall.

Hector ducks and rolls underneath a pirate's legs.

Wide-eyed, Buttercup watches with her heart in her throat. He's going to get hurt!

Hector dashes across to the horses and jumps on Windthrup. He grabs the reigns to the other horse and tosses the rope to Buttercup. "Here!" he yells.

As she tugs Forget-Me-Not closer she wonders where Hector got this spurt of courage. Hadn't he fainted in Ginglebop when she came out of the dragon? Buttercup doesn't have time to think of that now, though. She jumps up into the saddle and looks around the boat.

"Now what?" yells Hector.

She has the craziest idea, but it just might work. "Jump!" she yells.

The Pirates stumble back as Forget-Me-Not gallops towards them. Hector follows behind her on Windthrup. It looks like they are going to smash into all the weapons, but just in the nick of time, their horses jump over the pirates. They have leapt so far and high that they not only sail over the pirate's heads, but they sail over the side of the boat, too.

Hector is yelling.

The water is coming up faster and faster. Neither Buttercup nor Hector know how to swim!

She only has a moment to think. Then she gets an idea. The glass frog gave her a piece of glass to cut through the ropes, so maybe it can give them magic to breathe underwater!

Just as she thinks this they crash into the ocean.

SPLASH!

SilverWeed

Water goes into her mouth and nose.

She's scared. She's never swum before. Water is all around her, not allowing her to breathe!

Buttercup forces her eyes open. The glass frog and the glass ball are falling to the ocean floor.

She kicks her feet and swims towards them. Buttercup can't believe it. She's swimming! Reaching out with two hands she grabs both the glass objects. Buttercup needs to breathe. She's been under water too long.

She imagines what it must be like to be a fish and breathe in water. The glass frog and ball glow. And then she can breathe.

Oxygen fills her lungs and she smiles.

"Wow!" she says. She can talk underwater too!

Then she notices Hector. He's trying to swim, but is slowly sinking. Air bubbles travel up from his mouth.

She swims to him and gives Hector the glass ball. Now he can breathe, too, and the air bubbles disappear.

"Hector! We can breathe and talk!"

However, Hector is not smiling. He points to something behind Buttercup.

She spins around and sees both their horses struggling in the water. They kick their feet trying to get back to the surface for air.

She swims over and presses the glass frog against both of them. She imagines they can breathe underwater, too. And then the strangest thing happens. The horses shrink until they have turned into seahorses! The bags they carried have shrunk too.

"Buttercup, we need to get away! The net!" Hector yells, and starts kicking his legs.

She looks up to see a rope net sinking. The pirates are trying to capture them again! She kicks her legs and moves away just in time. She smiles; the pirates will be disappointed when they see their net is empty!

Buttercup and Hector, along with their two seahorses, swim farther into the ocean. She has only heard tales about the sea. The ocean is much different than what she thought it would be. This ocean is never-ending.

Soon they swim into a patch of kelp. The green leaves float up to try and reach the surface of the water, but are stopped because their roots hold them in the sand. They swim through the kelp watching in amazement as the sunlight makes beautiful patterns on the ocean floor.

Hector points to a crab. As their shadows pass over, it scurries under a rock in fright.

"It's like we're swimming through grass," Hector says in awe, as he pushes some kelp out of the way.

"You're right," Buttercup agrees. Then she notices two friends have joined them. Dolphins! She recognizes their arched backs, round noses, and knowing eyes from a drawing in one of her lesson books.

The dolphins bob their heads and swim close. One swims to Hector, and the other to Buttercup. She reaches out a hand, and the dolphin presses its nose to her palm. Buttercup smiles. She looks into its eyes, and for a moment she believes her dolphin is smiling.

"They're helping us!" Hector swishes by. He's holding his dolphin's fin, and it's pulling Hector out of the kelp forest.

Buttercup grabs hold of her dolphin's fin, and suddenly the kelp plants are brushing her cheeks as they swim through. Soon the kelp is behind them, and both dolphins slow down. She pats her dolphin. "Thank you." It nods its head as if it understood her.

"Buttercup!"

She looks up and sees Hector pointing.

Dolphins are not the only creatures in the ocean that have come to greet them. A merperson is floating a few feet away, watching them. Buttercup has never met a merperson before and she didn't think this is what they would look like.

The merperson has a tail of bright yellow scales. Her fingers are webbed, like a frog's. Her hair is seaweed. One eye is purple and the other is green.

"Who are you?" asks Buttercup.

"My name is SilverWeed. Buttercup, I welcome you to the city of Seaweed." She points to a coral castle behind her. It is magnificently large with tall towers and turrets.

"How do you know my name?" Buttercup asks.

SilverWeed smiles. "Every merperson can read

thoughts. That is one of our special powers that our crystal ball gives us." SilverWeed points to a giant shining glass ball. "That is our magical power source."

"Wow," says Hector. "It looks like the glass ball from Ginglebop, only much larger."

As Hector marvels at its size, SilverWeed fixes her purple and green eyes on Buttercup. "We are here to help you on your quest."

"How do we know you'll help us?" Buttercup asks. She thinks of the Pirates. She doesn't want the merpeople to capture her too!

SilverWeed explains. "We know of your travels to find your powers. You have fought your way through pirates, a formidable dragon, and a bleak desert. We are friends who may hold answers. You have only to open your ears and listen:

"What you seek, you have already found.

Courage you will gain and wisdom will surround.

A master knight will find his battleground,

And the other shall be crowned.

For all is written on the waves of the sea,

Should you only look and understand thee."

Buttercup repeats the words in her head. *A master knight will find his battleground, and the other shall be crowned.* Will Hector become a knight? Will he look like Knight Shire in metal armor with a dazzling sword? If so, what battle will Hector have to fight? Is she going to be crowned? Who and what is she going to be crowned for? Is the fortune a lie, or is it really going to come true?

She has so many questions, but before she can ask them, SilverWeed speaks.

"I can read your mind, and I know you have questions, but I cannot answer them. My job is to give you a hint to the future. I cannot tell you exactly what will happen; otherwise, you may find a way to change it. Now, I know you are both hungry and tired, and I believe a rest is needed. Please come with me to my city of Seaweed, where you can regain your strength, for your journey has only just begun."

❧ Acknowledgements ❧

This book would have never been possible without Lucy. Thank you for being the ham that you are and insisting on hearing a bed time story. Thank you to the teachers who instilled confidence in my writing and pushed me to expand my creative boundaries. My dear friend Amanda Coakley, I can't thank you enough for agreeing to help on a book that, at the time, was just an idea floating in creative space. Liesl Miller and Jacquie Fuller, you are both amazingly insightful. Without your help and encouragement the words in this book would not be so expertly crafted. To Lillian Ham, for always believing in my writing endeavors and for being the greatest best friend a laughoholic like me could wish for. Lastly, thank you to my parents. Without your support, guidance, and push for me to read at an early age I would definitely not have fallen into my love of writing. I thank each and every one of you for being there throughout all the ups and downs of this self-publishing chaos.

Entering the Human Realm Soon!

The Buttercup Adventures Volume Two: The Mythical Realms

Margaret Ellis Raymond

was born in Portland, Maine. She was awarded a Scholastic Art & Writing Honorary Mention for the New England District in 2012. Her hobbies include fencing, photography and a daily habit of laughing too much. She is pursuing a degree in Occupational Therapy. For more information on upcoming titles, or the author, please visit: http://margaretellisraymo.wix.com/mellisr

Amanda Coakley, currently a junior in college, has stacks of notebooks filled with doodles she thought at one point to throw away. Thankfully, they are still in her dorm room as evidence to her artistic growth. She hopes to one day own a studio to show the various mediums she works with.

CPSIA information can be obtained at www.ICGtesting.com
Printed in the USA
LVOW05s1927231015

459559LV00014B/69/P

9 780996 584418